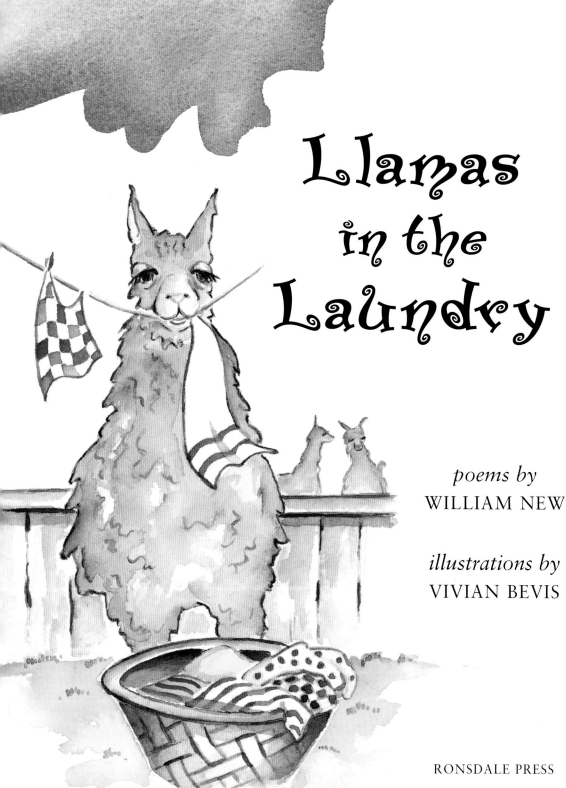

Llamas in the Laundry

poems by
WILLIAM NEW

illustrations by
VIVIAN BEVIS

RONSDALE PRESS

Soap Suds

Something I don't like a lot
Is soap that doesn't float,
'Cause when you have to have a bath
You want it for a boat,

Except it always sinks, and then
Your mother calls you out,
And when she pulls the plug
You hear her sputter,
            splash,
                  and shout:

Why did you leave the soap in the tub?
That's not what soap is for!
We are not sending soap to sea
Or washing Labrador!

I wonder if in Labrador
The fish take baths at sea,
And if they ever lose their soap
Where the plug should go, like me?

Tickle A Porcupine

Tickle a porcupine
Tickle his toes
Tickle and pickle a walrus's nose
Tickle a lobster
Tickle a clam
Tickle a bottle of blueberry jam
Tickle the tackle on top of a tug
Tickle the back of a barnacle bug
Tickle a prickly porcupine
All the way to the Argentine

Bigbat Littlebat

Bigbat littlebat brownbat boat
Kitten in a cupboard in a camelhair coat
Jump in Junebug
Jump out Jake
Kitten in the kitchen
Chocolate cake

Everyday Weekday

Findley Fundy Sydney Sunday
Courtenay Kootenay Calgary Monday
Goose Bay Tuesday
Glace Bay Wednesday
Burnaby Thursday
Gaspé Friday
Gimli Galloway Ogilvie Saturday
North Bay Little Bay Saguenay Sunday

MON TUES WED THURS FRI SAT

Counter-Berry Tale

Bramble amble thimbleberry
Tumble bumblebee
Grumble at a loganberry
ONE   TWO   THREE

Raspberry gooseberry
Stacks stalks sticks
Hay merry strawberry
FOUR   FIVE   SIX

Knock a nickel huckleberry
Walk a wicker wren
SEVEN   cyber-salmonberry
EIGHT   NINE   TEN

Ride A Rocket Round Regina

Ride a rocket round Regina
Ride a rocket to the moon
Take a parrot in your pocket
And a maple macaroon
Take your cousin's ukulele
And your crazy cousin too
Ride a rocket round Regina
Ride a rocket to the zoo

Wishing

Wombat platypus
    Joey kangaroo
I wish I had a pocketknife
    Just for you
I'd carve a wooden whistle
    From a weeping willow tree
And I'd whistle for a platypus
    To play with me.

Rhinos In Nanaimo

In August on my birthday
      I am going to be four —
And I know lots already
      like how cats get out the door —

My sister tells me acrobats
      can fly on Hallowe'en —
She tells me that in Paraguay
      the sky is apple green —

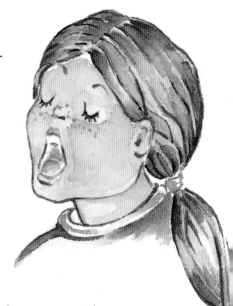

She says that no-one's hungry
      where spaghetti bushes grow —
She says when trains run out of gas
      the drivers have to row —

And she should know I guess because
      she's almost nearly nine —
And been as far as Duncan
      on the Island Railway Line —

But there is something she can't say —
    (I know she knows that I know) —
She cannot say Rhinoceroses
    wriggle in Nanaimo! —

She grumbles Rhinosauceros —
    she mumbles Maraschino —
Rhinonneruss in rustybus —
    Renosterous in Reno —

And specially she splutters
    if I chance to say The Rhino
giggles wiggles jiggles squiggles
    wriggles in Nanaimo!

Llamas In The Llaundry

Llamas in the llaundry
Llamas in the llane
Llamas smellll of llavender
Grandma's on the pllane.

Llamas in the kitchen
Llamas in a clloud
Llamas wearing lleotards
Grandma llaughs lloud.

Llamas in the valllley
Llamas on the hillll
Llamas llicking llollllipops
Grandma's here stillll.

Llamas in the Andes
Llamas in Peru
Llamas llive on llemonade
Grandma lloves you.

Jen-Gerbil

Oh, I love my grandpa,
  My grandpa loves me;
He calls me Jen-Gerbil-
  Jen-Ginger-McGee.

He reads me his stories,
  I sit on his knee,
  and he whispers,
    "Jen-Gerbil-
      Jen-Ginger-McGee,

Do you know that tomorrow's
a mountain so high
and so covered in berries
the colour of sky

that only small gerbils
who nibble the night
into paperbark dreams
of mulberry light

can see to the top
of the very next day?"

"Oh, Grandpa, you're telling
a story," I say.

But he smiles, and softly
blows kisses to me,
saying,
"Gerbil, Jen-Gerbil-
Jen-Ginger-McGee."

Wild Horses

In France and Spain and Italy
Wild horses race beside the sea;
Beside the sea they toss their manes
Like open-ocean weathervanes.

In Spain and Italy and France
Wild horses toss their heads and dance,
Dance to music they alone
Can hear above the ocean's moan.

In Italy and France and Spain
Wild horses neigh along the main;
They fly before the wind and neigh
To race the waves and tidal spray.

They kick against the weathered sand;
They ride the ragged rim of land;
Around the world they seem to fly
Against the ocean-coloured sky.

When I was little I could fling
Along with them, and dance and sing:
But now I watch them race the sea
In France and Spain and Italy.

Zoo

My sister has a rattlesnake,
  My brother has a rat,
    My other sister's boa
      wraps itself around her hat.

    The boa's pretty lazy,
      The rat's a runaway,
        The rattlesnake is noisy
          as the rain in Thunder Bay.

        The rat smells like my brother,
          My sister bites her nails,
            My other sister stretches like
              a sack of soggy snails.

I'll tell you why my guinea pig,
my goldfish, dog, and cat
all stay outside to bawl and bark
and burble, burp, and blat:

The other pets — the wildest —
give them and me the blisters
(The wildest are the ones inside:
My brother and my sisters).

My Parents' Friends

My Mum and Dad have fourteen friends —
our house is wild when they descend —
    They're always saying how I've grown
    and act as if my anklebones
    had somehow grown beyond my socks —
They gush and feint and shadow box
then start to pant and soon ignore me
(one of them is nearly forty) —

But they don't realize I see
much more of them than they see me —
      One eats only sweet confections —
      One wears stripes in all directions —
Two are wider than they're tall
and puff about The Wherewithal
when they're together — I admit
I stretch the truth by just a bit

but not a lot — Another two
I think would make a kangaroo
a little tense — They twitch and jump
every time they hear a thump —

Three wear cell phones on their hip
(I think they're in a Partnership
and call each other up) — There's one
who claims to dye her hair for fun —
it's sometimes blue and sometimes green —
And one who smells of gasoline —

One is skinny — One wears plaid
(he's the brother of my Dad) —
And one who perches when she eats
(she keeps a pair of parakeets) —

And all of them are sort of nice
if you can stand their weird advice —

They kiss and everlastingly
keep asking what I want to be —

I tell them what they want to hear —
An Astronaut, An Auctioneer —
        But that's not quite the truth — If I
        were honest, I'd say Dragonfly —
But I am shy — If I were bolder
This is what I'd tell them: Older.

There Is Porridge On The Ceiling

There is porridge on the ceiling
of my science class — it's peeling
all the paint off all the walls
and it's seeping down the halls
beneath the tiles on the floor
and it's creeping up the door —
congealing on the windowpanes,
concealing boards and stealing brains —

it is mushing every room,
consuming air and I assume
it's taking over — all my friends
are keeling over with the bends,
and the teacher's looking grim,
I think it's got a hold of him —
and it's now approaching me,
it's nearer than it ought to be,
it will turn me into glue —

oh —
        I know what to do:
The question isn't hard at all,
I know the answer after all —

and the porridge stops its gnawing,
it's revolving, it's withdrawing,
it's dissolving, disappearing,
and I think the air is clearing —

(I'm very glad I have to say
This doesn't happen every day)

Auntie Calamity Sank Through The Floor

Icicle bicycle popsicle pig
Auntie Calamity put on a wig —
    The wig was so heavy she started to sink
    in a barrel of purply polkadot ink —

Down went her left foot
Down went her right
Down when her anklebone slipped out of sight —
    But she straightened her wig,
    gave her parting a pat,
    and standing up vertical, reached for her hat —

Icicle bicycle conical cat
Auntie Calamity put on her hat —
    The hat was as big as a bucket of cheese
    and Auntie Calamity sank to her knees:
        She sank to her middle
        and sank a bit more,

She reached for the ribbon that hung on the door,
    She wrapped a red handkerchief under her chin,
    attached a blue bow with a surgical pin —

Icicle bicycle fudgicle foe
Auntie Calamity put on her bow:
    She sank from her neck to her uppermost earring —
    Winked at the world just before disappearing —
        But that's not the end of this story —
        there's more:
        Auntie Calamity sank through the floor —

She asked for a crane to come by the next day
to help her up out of the basement to play —

And that's all there is — except we play now
Icicle bicycle cubical cow
    With her wig in a bag in a box by the bed
       and all of the bicycles out in the shed.

Sandwishes

I'm hungry, an hour's
  gone by since my lunch —
I think that I'll make me
  a sandwich to munch —
I'll start with the bread —
  two slices of rye,
one for the bottom
  and one for up high —
and then for the middle
  I think that I'll add
lettuce, and yoghurt
  that hasn't gone bad —

a piece of fried liver
    that's gone through a shredder,
some broccoli bits
    and a layer of cheddar,
42 gherkins
    in licorice custard,
marshmallow, marmalade,
    melon, and mustard —
a dollop of eggplant,
    a scoop of zucchini,
asparagus salsa,
    a green jelly bean,
and if that's not enough
    then I'll need to add honey,
cereal flakes,
    and an egg that's still runny,
a ripe avocado,
    some leftover beans,
a 43rd pickle,
    and seven sardines —
bits of green spinach
    and ripe macaroni,
cabbage and carrots,
    a slice of bologna,
with olives and oysters

and one onion ring,
morsels of brussels sprouts,
      corn à la king,
a chunk of banana,
      a hunk of potato,
pepper and salt,
      and a lump of tomato —
bubblegum ice cream
      to give it a glaze —
oh, I almost forgot:
      the soy mayonnaise —
then interleaved layers
      of turnip and jam
till the sandwich is almost
      as tall as I am —

and then I'll just add
     some whipped cream and a cherry,
and I shall be full
     until dinnertime. Nearly.

RONSDALE PRESS
3350 West 21st Avenue
Vancouver, B.C. Canada V6S 1G7
www.ronsdalepress.com

Typesetting: Julie Cochrane, Vancouver, BC
Printing: King's Time, Hong Kong

Ronsdale Press wishes to thank the Canada Council for the Arts, the Government of Canada through the Book Publishing Industry Development Program (BPIDP), and the Province of British Columbia through the British Columbia Arts Council for their support of its publishing program.

NATIONAL LIBRARY OF CANADA CATALOGUING IN PUBLICATION DATA
New, W.H. (William Herbert), 1938–
Llamas in the laundry

Poems
ISBN 0-921870-97-3

1. Canada—Juvenile poetry. I. Bevis, Vivian, 1937–   II. Title.
PS8577.E776L52 2002   jC811'.54   C2002-910102-6
PR9199.3.N395L52 2002